DANIEL NESQUENS & MAGICOMORA

MY TATTOOED DAD

Translated by Elisa Amado

GROUNDWOOD BOOKS · HOUSE OF ANANSI PRESS
TORONTO   BERKELEY

Dad goes and comes. Like the day, like the night.

When you least expect him, swoosh, you'll find him digging in the garden, pulling out weeds that have grown up all over the place. Or he'll be in the kitchen, wearing an apron, making dinner as though he hasn't just been away for more than two months.

Mom looks at him happily and kisses his neck while he fries up those chicken samosas that I love. He lights some incense and the smell fills the house. We eat dinner and he makes jokes and I play a few tricks on him. Dad loves to play the fool. When my eyes start to feel heavy, he picks me up and carries me off to bed.

In the quiet dawn I feel someone giving me a kiss. It prickles a bit. I think maybe it's a dream. But, no. When I wake up in the morning Dad isn't there. Mom says he's gone, leaving us alone together once again.

"Dad's got ants in his pants," says Mom.

Maybe that's the only place he doesn't have a tattoo. Because Dad has tattoos all over, from his head to his toes. Arms, shoulders, back, chest, wrists, hands, thighs — as I said, from his head to his toes. Reading his tattoos is more fun than reading any book ever written.

Tigers, elephants, gorillas, winding serpents, magical birds, spiders … faces, firecrackers, crazy machines … they cover his whole body.

"Put your finger in its mouth. You'll feel it bite,"
Dad said one day, showing me a tiger with two tails
tattooed on his forearm.

Without stopping to think I put my

finger where he said, and felt a prick.

I jumped and Dad laughed his huge laugh that you can hear right through
the wall.

"Why has it got two tails?" I asked.

"Oh, well, no one knows. What I do know is that it almost tore my arm off."
He sat back and went on with his story.

A huge storm had driven us off course. The sky was like lead, and there was
a suffocating smell of tar.

The ship ran aground on a coral reef near an island. I figured it must be
The Island of the Sea Monkey so we decided to go ashore in our dinghy. But
when we stepped onto firm ground there was not a sound to be heard. No
birds sang, no monkeys rustled in the bushes. We were worried. We pushed
into that dark, impenetrable jungle until suddenly we came upon a ruined
Portuguese fort. All that remained were some burned timbers and a
skeleton hanging from a bare branch. Its bones were held together by string
so that it looked like a marionette.

And all of a sudden the bones began to come apart one by one, as though
an invisible hand was cutting the string.

The bones fell like rain until they formed the shape of a skull on the
ground. Herbert James, our captain, clutched his hands to his head and
cried, "It's the curse of Pim, the warrior who was reborn as a tiger." He
threw away his musket and tore off like a soul pursued by the devil himself.

PIM TIGER

My old friend Samson joined his hands in prayer. But it didn't do him any good because a magnificent tiger with gleaming black stripes appeared out of nowhere and leapt upon him.

In a flash it tore off poor Samson's head. The headless body ran off until it crashed into a tree and fell to the ground.

Pim Tiger, who was at least three meters tall, sniffed at the head and pushed it away. Then it turned and stared at me. Red veins like rivers ran through its eyes.

I had no time to act. Pim Tiger jumped on me and we rolled over and over on the ground, hugging each other like lovers. I don't know how many times we rolled but I felt like a stuffed toy in its terrible claws. I heard an almost unearthly roar in my ears as it ripped a big chunk off my scalp.

I don't know how I finally managed to land a right hook, but for the beast it was just a tickle. When I tried a left hook it just grabbed my wrist and broke it. We kept rolling around until suddenly Pim Tiger let out a blood-curdling roar, as though it had been shot by a lightning bolt, and dropped me immediately.

I jumped up and saw that Samson's head had somehow got Pim Tiger's tails in its jaws. The tiger kept wheeling around trying to free its tails from the terrible grip of those teeth. But it couldn't.

I couldn't help it. I began to roar with laughter. Ha! Ha! Ha!

Pim Tiger ran back into the jungle with Samson's head still attached to its tails.

And that was the last time my dear old friend ever did me a favor.

"You could spend hours and hours, and you'd never guess what Samson's job was," said my dad.

I shrugged.

"Come on, guess."

"Sailor?"

"Yes, of course he was a sailor for a while. But I mean before he joined the ship and we sailed halfway around the world."

"Baker? Farmer?"

"No."

"Electrician? Plumber? Carpenter?"

"No, no, no."

"Doctor? Lawyer? Architect?"

"Not at all, not at all."

"I give up," I said.

Old Samson spent three-quarters of his life as the zookeeper in Woking. He was in charge of caring for the animals. His favorite was an elephant named Mahler, like the composer. It wasn't a very big zoo but there was a lot of work.

As his workload grew heavier, Samson realized that he was getting very tired. One day a snake bit one of his fingers, which from then on was as stiff as a broom handle. That disaster made him think seriously about his future. He finally made up his mind when one of the gorillas almost managed to sink its fangs into his face, a misfortune that was prevented in the nick of time by a zoo visitor.

This near-miss left a small, almost invisible mark on his cheek.

Old Samson liked to while away the warm nights on the high seas telling us stories about his friend Mahler. How he would stretch out his trunk and eat a whole wheelbarrow full of oranges. How he could recognize himself in a mirror. How one day Mahler grabbed Samson and spun him around like a pinwheel. Or how, one summer morning, the elephant stretched his trunk way out and snatched a cone with three scoops of chocolate ice cream from a red-headed boy who was walking by with his mother. The day he told us that story was the first time I had seen old Samson smile in a very long time.

Dad's eyes were closed and his mouth was slightly open.

"Dad?"

"Yes, son?"

"Did you know that elephants are the only animals that can't jump?"

"Like old Samson. He couldn't jump either. And all because his friend Mahler stepped on his foot and reduced the bones to crumbs."

Dad sighed deeply and stared at the toes of his shoes.

On the other side of town the factories were quiet. You could tell it was a holiday.

It had been raining very hard and there were pud-
dles in the street. I was looking out my bedroom
window. The mailman rang the bell and dropped
an envelope in the mailbox. I went downstairs half
dressed. The envelope was so covered with stamps
that there was barely room for the address. But
there in Dad's handwriting was my name in capital
letters. I tore it open and read:

Congratulations. Soon it will be your

birthday. I'm not sure I can be at home to pull your ears. In case I'm not,
I'm sending you this present. I hope you like it. This is my lucky card.
I don't think I need it anymore. But take good care of it as I have. You'll
notice that it's kind of singed. That's the trace of gunpowder.

I'm also sending the brooch that your mother lost the day she first held my
hand. I just found it yesterday. It's so strange. Many years have passed, but
I'm certain that this is that very brooch.

I remember as if it were yesterday. We went to a traveling circus that was
visiting all the greatest cities of the world. It was my first date with your
mother. Before the show we took a little walk. We weren't paying attention
to where we were going and suddenly we came upon an old wagon that gave
off a very special light. We peered in the window and saw an old woman
looking into a crystal ball. She turned and stared at us.

The door swung open and a carpet of light showed us the way in. We
climbed the steps. Our shadows filled the doorway.

"It's been ten years since I've spoken to anyone," she said in greeting. "I was waiting for you."

"The door was open," I stammered. Your mother grabbed my hand.

"Sit down," said the old woman, and she placed her hands firmly on the ball.

The linoleum was dirty and a bit uneven. One of the walls was half covered with a picture of a man holding down a devil by the arm.

"Young lady, you are blessed by the Goddess of Destiny," said the old woman. "You will have a son named Pierre. You...you two are not of this world. Things will happen that you can't imagine. This very night something will take place that you will remember forever."

She held out her hands. They were as wrinkled as old paper. She swallowed and added, "Everything depends on you. Take one of these cards and now, go away."

I took the card that you have in your hand and we left the wagon. The light went out. Your mother was still holding onto me. Without saying a word, we let our feet lead us to the circus entrance. The doorman bowed when he saw the card and called over his strange little assistant who led us to our seats.

The performance had begun. A beautiful Amazon was standing on the bare back of a handsome white horse. Then the ringmaster made way for a man wearing a black vest.

He pulled it open and we saw that he had a pistol. He pulled it out, pointed at the roof and fired. Petals rained down on the audience.

"Anna," he cried, and a stunning woman came into the ring.

She tied a kerchief around his eyes and went and stood before a board and spread her arms wide. The gunslinger began to shoot in her direction. The bullets did not touch her, though they made an outline around her body.

"Now for the last shot!" called the man, and he turned and aimed right at where your mother and I were sitting.

People screamed. He had gone crazy.

He let out a wild laugh and pulled the trigger...

BANG!

I was still holding the card. I threw it down and grabbed that terrible bullet. You've seen for yourself the scorch mark on the palm of my hand. The gunman took off and disappeared into the crowd. As you can imagine the audience was crazy with fright, and people were screaming and running in circles. We heard a shot nearby. Someone yelled that the tiger with two tails had escaped. The crowd was so wild that a thief made off with some wallets and a brooch...

But no one was harmed.

By pure chance I found the brooch yesterday, inside a fish, just like in "The Little Lead Soldier" by Hans Christian Andersen. Luckily I hadn't yet sealed this envelope that you have just opened.

Congratulations, son. You are almost a man.

It was nice under the apple tree. The smell of wood smoke floated gently in the air.

Dad opened his mouth and pulled out a bird. He perched it on my hand and said, "It's for you. Its name is Bird."

"Bird? Just Bird?" I asked.

He nodded, opened his mouth and began to talk.

It was the first day of autumn. The sun shone on the mountain. It was much steeper than I'd imagined. Everything looked different than it had from down below. The cliff leaned over me and there were hardly any handholds on the rock face.

As I climbed, the sky seemed to loom closer. The wind began to blow. Suddenly a cloud moved in and covered me and it began to rain. A lightning bolt struck the rock just a hand's breadth away. I could almost reach out and grab it.

Then I saw a nest perfectly clearly. There was a chick in it and it was all alone. That chick was almost your size, son. It was swallowing a worm as long as a crochet hook.

The people in the valley were very superstitious. They had told me about the condemned souls and invisible cities among the mountain peaks. But I just had to reach out and grab that chick. I set aside all thought of the spirits and invisible genies that were supposedly guarding the place. It was all just talk, I told myself.

I put my foot on an outcropping but it broke off. Then I was hanging by one hand, and I could feel something dragging me down. At that moment I was closer to dying than living. Only three fingers were keeping me alive. I fell…

…into the void. I was a dead man when something grabbed me in its large curved talons. I turned my head and saw a white-breasted albatross. It was gigantic. And it was carrying me as though I were nothing but a shopping bag filled with yogurt cups.

The giant bird soared over the valley. The river below looked like a snake. Huge trees were no bigger than capital I's. We flew through a mint-flavored cloud, swooping in circles.

I was getting dizzy. We kept circling until we reached the nest where its chick was squawking and calling. The albatross dropped me into the bone-filled nest. The chick opened its beak and I could see that it had a forked tongue like a serpent. Its yellow eyes stared at me.

That's when my good luck kicked in, just like magic. A ray of sunshine bounced off my ring, blinding the chick.

I didn't think twice. I threw myself out into space like a winged angel. But I didn't need wings. I just flew.

If what I'm saying isn't true, tell me how on earth I could be here with you now, telling you this story under this beautiful apple tree?

Dad felt in his pockets but found nothing. He finished his tea in a gulp and left the cup balancing on the saucer. It wobbled.

As I was saying…it was good under that apple tree.

According to my father, I've nearly died twice.
The first time was when a wild dog stole me as I was
quietly sleeping in my baby basket.

Mom and Dad were watching a robin chirping and
hopping about, when it suddenly began to flap its wings. Dad turned and
saw a mutt carrying me off in its jaws. Mom fainted and Dad set off running after it. But the dog was faster than he was and kept getting farther and
farther ahead.

When he realized he couldn't catch up, Dad stopped dead. He panted, then
used his hands as a megaphone.

"Hey, you, Clic-Clac. Why are you called Clic-Clac? Let's make a deal."

The dog stopped and turned its head.

"Give me the baby and I'll teach you how to fish."

The dog ran on.

"Whatever, Clic-Clac. But that creature isn't worth much. Can't you feel how light it is? It won't even begin to fill your stomach. And as soon as you put it down, it will start to bawl and wail. It's a crybaby. It will drive you crazy. It won't do a thing for you. Bring it back and I'll show you how to fish. There's bone fish in the river. Its flesh is dark and sweeter than anything, and its bones taste like cinnamon..."

The dog looked at my dad, then over at the river. It sniffed the air. Dad started to walk up to it.

"Listen to the burbling of the water, Clic-Clac. The bone fish is a dark fish with a big flat body. It's from the acantoptigenous family. It only eats puppini, trumpetoni, birdingae and islemouths..."

The dog, bewitched by my father's words, dropped me on the ground.

"You have to fish for them at dawn, with the wax of bee larvae. When they open up the dam you can catch them easily, two by two. Or even three by three...I'll show you." My father's heart was beating furiously. "Look how dirty your ears are. I'll have to wash them with the hose. Come on, let's go home. Good boy, Clic-Clac..."

The second time I nearly died was coming back from my grandparents' house. I flew out the car window just as it was going around one of those endless highway curves. My father sped up and began to drive like a real race car driver. A thousand kilometers an hour. The tires squealed and everything in the car flew from side to side. Passing a tight curve on the left, Dad reached out the window and opened his hand, and I fell right in.

My father had saved me from flying into a rocky wall.

The next day was my birthday. I don't remember which one. Maybe two, or maybe less.

That night it rained so hard that we wondered if we should all learn to swim.

The potholes were so deep that a

double-decker bus might disappear in them. I opened my bedroom window a bit and yawned at the clouds. My stomach was rumbling. It was time for breakfast.

As I went down to the kitchen I saw that the door to my parents' bedroom was closed. That was unusual. I could hear voices.

Holding my breath, I held my ear to the door, like a Russian spy. It was my mother who was talking.

"Can I know what's gotten into you?"

"Excuse me, madam, but I don't know you."

It was definitely my father's voice.

"Not know me? I'm your wife!"

"My wife? Ha, ha. I don't have a wife!"

"What kind of joke is that?"

"It's not a joke. Now, if you'll allow me, I'll go home."

"Just a minute. You are home. And you're not leaving until this is cleared up."

The voices were getting closer. What was happening in there?

"I beg you to move away from the door unless...unless you want..."

I heard a bang, and the door suddenly opened. Dad stared at me as if he had never seen me before. His bottom lip, bruised and kind of swollen, was trembling, making his words sound weird.

"And you, young man, are you going to tell me what you are doing here instead of guarding the entrance to the cave?

Now that the treasure chest has disappeared I can tell you that you're going to be piranha food. When did you abandon your post? Answer me, boy!"

My throat burned. The veins were beating in my head. My tongue felt like a stick of charcoal.

What was happening to my father? What should I say?

Then Dad tightened his lips, as though lightning had struck him in the stomach, and he bent over and started to cough violently.

His cough became a plume of smoke, as if he'd been smoking a cigar. Then something like molten lava poured out and swirled around our feet. It was followed by flaming black rocks. Dad's face was bright red. The rocks came crashing down and made holes in the floor.

"Hello, son. What are you doing up so early? Whew, I just dreamt that I swallowed Stromboli."*

He gave me a hard pat on the back.

"Now everyone, time for breakfast. My stomach is empty. I'd love a great big piece of toast slathered with butter and apricot jam."

My mother sat next to me and patted my knee. All you could see in the breadbasket was a little triangle of burnt bread. It looked just like an erupting volcano.

*Stromboli is a volcano in Italy.

My father sighed.

I was admiring a flame tree. Someone had told me that flame trees represent a passing fancy, a brief passion…

I was trying to remember who had

said that when something thumped me on the back. I turned my head but didn't see anyone.

The thumps came again. I looked up and discovered a huge hairy ball hanging over me. A city could have fit in its shadow.

It was a spider made of bits of other spiders. Its eyes were bottomless wells. Its belly was the color of the flowers on the flame tree — deep, orangey-red. From its mouth hung a small alligator. Yes, an alligator. It opened its mouth and the alligator fell out.

Then the spider spoke to me in a voice that pierced right through me.

"It's a nice tree, isn't it? Too bad its flowers wilt so quickly. And too bad I don't like the seedpods. I only eat fresh meat. My favorite is human meat. Have you ever eaten human meat?"

No words came. I shook my head. My ears were buzzing. I tried to think of how to get away but I couldn't.

I was edging under it so that its eyes wouldn't be able to see me, when its belly opened and another blood-stained eye popped out as if it were on a spring.

FLAME TREE

"I asked if you've ever eaten human meat? Yes? No? Sometimes?"

"No, no, I haven't eaten it," I answered.

"Would you like to try some? A hand, for example. No, not a hand. Too bony. An ear? This ear? What a delicacy. A delicious ear. How mouth-watering. Heh, heh, heh."

One of its legs bent and grabbed me around the waist, bringing me right up to that dreadful eye. Another leg bent. One of its sharp nails seemed close to my ear.

"The secret lies in the cut. It has to be clean. Right behind the ear lobe. Heh, heh, heh."

I felt something sharp sliding behind my ear. I moved just enough to keep it from cutting me, and the knife slipped and cut one of the beast's own feet.

A horrible green jelly-like liquid began to flow. Drawn by the hot smell, an army of red ants began to move down the branches of the flame tree. In less than half a minute a million ants swarmed over the giant spider, which suddenly dropped me. I heard various things fall to the ground. I could see and not see. The ants ate the spider in silence.

Not a hair of the disgusting creature remained.

The red ants, slightly swollen, went back to their nest single file. I took a deep breath and fainted.

When I woke up, I was lying in the shade of that wonderful tropical tree.

My father sighed again.

9

When I went into that store I didn't yet know your mother.

A bell tinkled and from the back of the store came a man dressed in an impeccable black suit that he wore over a black shirt buttoned right to the collar. On his head was a top hat that didn't go with the suit at all. The man could not have been more than half a meter tall.

Until he jumped onto the counter all I could see of him was the crown of his hat. He only reached up to my chin.

"Good morning," I said. "I'd like — " But he raised a finger to his lips.

"Ssssh! Say no more. I know what's brought you to this store. You want to meet the mouse that belled the cat."*

I was so surprised that I lifted my eyebrows. The man reached into his pocket and pulled out a mouse that he placed on the counter. It looked at me, stood on its hind legs and held itself as stiff as a porcelain figurine.

"Now I want to meet the cat," I demanded.

I heard the tinkling of a bell. A cat almost as big as the man, with big oval eyes, peered around a corner and stared at the terrified mouse.

"I hate it," said the cat, and then he vanished. The man smiled and pulled a pocket watch out of his jacket.

"Oh, it's my breakfast time. A delicious cup of tea with bran toast and a soft-boiled egg. Will you join me?"

I didn't know what to say. It all seemed too strange.

"Are you coming or not?"

I nodded.

"Did the cat that was belled by the mouse get your tongue, or what?" he laughed.

*From Aesop's fable, "Belling the Cat"

The man took off his hat and laid it on the counter. He put in his hand and…didn't take anything out. He sighed loudly and tried again. Sweat popped out on his brow.

Nothing.

"Can you please put your arm in? Mine doesn't reach to the bottom. Every day it's shorter, like my life."

The man held out his hat and I put my hand in, blindly. I pulled out a tea pot, a delicate porcelain tea cup, some toast, a chunk of cheese, half a banana, an apple, two kiwis, three kumquats, four dried figs…and I don't know what else.

But there was no egg. The man was becoming impatient. He crossed his arms on his chest.

"The egg…the egg is missing. Look carefully. It must be in there. Every day of my life I've breakfasted on a cup of tea, bran toast and a soft-boiled egg," he said.

"Wouldn't two slices of tomato do?" I asked, showing them to him.

"No, I don't want that."

And he growled, just like Pim Tiger. A deep growl that ended in a kind of grunt mixed with a dry cough.

"Princess, can you come out here, please?" he called.

And she did.

Dad stopped. He lifted his eyebrows and smiled happily for a moment. "In eight seconds the train will go by," he said, looking at the clock.

"Eight, seven, six, five…"

We both looked out the window.

"…three, two, one…"

And at that exact moment the express train roared past, on time, as always.

The train had passed but the story was only
half over.

Dad leaned back in his chair.

I imagine he was counting the seconds before I would open my mouth.
Three, two, one...

"Are you saying that Mom was working in that store?" I asked.

"No, no. As far as I know she never worked in a store."

"Then who was it who appeared when the man in the top hat called out
'Princess?'"

"No, no. Princess appeared, all right. But she wasn't your mother. She was
a serpent. An anaconda covered in brilliant scales whose coils went on and
on. She slithered in silently, bending and swaying. Like a little whirlwind
she quickly wound herself around my leg and wrapped herself around my
arms. I couldn't move. When she reached my neck, she stretched out into
the air. She reached toward the man and opened her mouth. Her forked
tongue came out and on it lay two eggs. The man took them.

"Mmm. Thanks, Princess. How kind. I can see that you would like our
customer to join us. But first I must cook these beautiful eggs. For that I
shall repair to the kitchen. It will take exactly three minutes. Don't move,
young man."

He went into the back of the store. And there I was all alone, unable
to move.

"Did you know that according to the aboriginal people of Australia, when the world began the serpents were in charge of creating the rivers? That's why rivers have so many curves. Their beds are like the bending shapes of serpents," said the man from the back of the store.

Princess looked at me with her bulging eyes and I looked back. I was afraid.

"They also say that serpents dug the wells so they could rest in them. That's why they're round. When the dry season comes they climb into the wells and live down there. That's why you have to be careful —"

I didn't hear anything else. It was as though night had suddenly fallen. It was totally dark, without a sliver of moonlight.

Princess had swallowed me whole in one gulp, from head to toe.

A sound
like a
motor sur-
rounded me.
Her insides were
slimy. I remembered
the Bible story about
Jonah, who lived for three days
and three nights inside a whale.* But I wasn't in a whale. I was in an anaconda that was in a store run by a man who was in the back cooking two eggs
that were probably in a saucepan. Inside.

But I wanted to be out. Outside.

I'd never been in such an extreme situation. I felt around with my hand.

*From the book of the prophet Jonah in the Bible

SERPENT

I pinched myself to make sure I wasn't dead.

But, no. I wasn't. Princess had been kind enough not to suffocate me. She'd swallowed me alive.

"Thanks a lot, Princess," I whispered.

And then I sneezed. My sneeze caused a light to appear. Shining sparks hung in the air like comets. And I saw a frightened white rabbit hiding behind a mandrake root. And a dove that flew around without stopping. And a hen that pecked without lifting her head. And a cartoon mouse. And a dog with its tongue hanging out. And a two-tailed tiger. And a headless man running. And a minotaur desperately trying to escape...

I leaned over and picked up a stone. I split it in two. I blew on the split and an echo appeared.

"Over there!" it called. And I ran and ran until I found the way out.

Outside, it was a bright clear day. Spring-like. I walked to the train station and bought myself a ticket to somewhere.

"Have a good trip," said the ticket man.

There were still ten minutes to go before the train. So I sat in front of a redhead who was reading a book.

She put the book on the bench. She raised her head and looked at me. We smiled.

The train went by but neither of us moved.

We walked into town together.

A traveling circus was just getting ready to put up the big top.

There are many days when Mom rocks in her chair and stares into space. I'm sure she's thinking about Dad, wondering whether he's all right, whether something bad has happened to him.

There are many nights when I lie in bed, sorting out Dad's stories. But they get all tangled up, like a ball of wool that someone has dropped. Time passes and I end up leaving them just the way they came into my mind. Tangled.

When I was little I thought Dad was in charge of hanging the moon in the sky. Now I know that's not true. But sometimes, on nights when he's out there, he does hang up a star.

That one, for example.

MY ★ TATTOOED ★ DAD

Papá Tatuado, text by Daniel Nesquens
and illustrations by Sergio Mora
Original edition copyright © 2009 by A Buen Paso,
Barcelona, Spain, www.abuenpaso.es
English translation copyright © 2011 by Elisa Amado
First published in English in Canada and the USA in 2011 by
Groundwood Books

The rights to this book were negotiated through
Sea of Stories Literary Agency, www.seaofstories.com,
Sidonie@seaofstories.com.

Groundwood Books / House of Anansi Press
110 Spadina Avenue, Suite 801, Toronto, Ontario M5V 2K4
or c/o Publishers Group West
1700 Fourth Street, Berkeley, CA 94710

We acknowledge for their financial support of our
publishing program the Government of Canada through the
Canada Book Fund (CBF).

Library and Archives Canada Cataloguing in Publication
Nesquens, Daniel
My tattooed dad / Daniel Nesquens ; Magicomora,
illustrator ; Elisa Amado; translator.
Translation of: Papá tatuado.
ISBN 978-1-55498-109-0
I. Amado, Elisa II. Mora, Sergio III. Title.
PZ7.N4383My 2011   j863'.7   C2010-905910-7

The illustrations are pencil drawings that have been scanned
and colored digitally.
Design by orecchio acerbo

Printed and bound in China